LUCKY TUCKER

Leslie McGuirk

WALKER BOOKS
AND SUBSIDIARIES
LONDON · BOSTON · SYDNEY · AUCKLAND

This book is dedicated to
Susan Welter — a human good-luck charm.

When Tucker woke up on Saint Patrick's Day,
he got off on the wrong paw.

First he had to go for a walk in the rain ... BEFORE breakfast.

Then his favourite squeaky toy got stuck under the sofa.

Just when he thought it couldn't get
any worse, a black cat hissed at him!

My luck needs to change, thought Tucker.

What if I ...

roll in this bed of clover?
Maybe some luck will rub off on me.

Little did he know that he was
being watched by a leprechaun!

"You just rolled in my bed of four-leaf clover!" the leprechaun said. "Now you'll be the luckiest dog around!"

And off he ran.

Tucker chased after the leprechaun. But he got sidetracked when he saw a boy licking an ice cream. The top scoop was about to fall off!

Tucker caught it!
"Wow, what a lucky dog," the boy said.

By now the leprechaun had disappeared,
so Tucker decided to go to the park.

Today WAS his lucky day! He got to play and wrestle with all his best friends.

On his way home, Tucker passed by the bakery that sold homemade dog biscuits.

"This is your lucky day, Tucker!" said the baker.

 "I've got a peanut-butter shamrock,

 a chicken-flavoured pot of gold

and

 a cheese-flavoured horseshoe
just for you!"

When Tucker arrived home, the
postman was delivering a big box.

Tucker tore open the box and jumped inside.

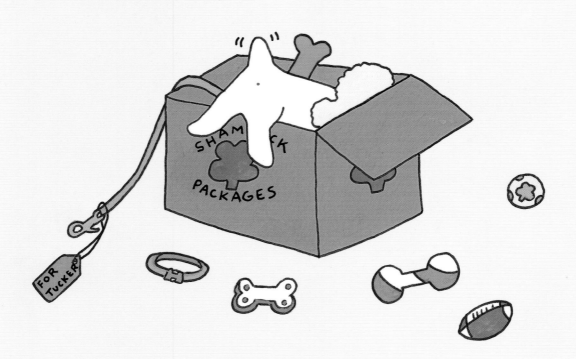

His owner said, "Lucky Tucker, you were supposed to have a bath tonight, but let's play with your new toys instead!"

Finally, it was time for Tucker to go to bed.
It HAD been his luckiest day ever!

And he was already dreaming about next Saint Patrick's Day ...

First published 2008 by Walker Books Ltd
87 Vauxhall Walk, London SE11 5HJ

2 4 6 8 10 9 7 5 3 1

This book is handlettered by Leslie McGuirk

Printed in China

British Library Cataloguing in Publication Data:
a catalogue record for this book is available from the British Library

ISBN 978-1-4063-1398-7

www.walkerbooks.co.uk